The MUPPET MOVIE

front cover photographed by NANCY MORAN/DONAL HOLWAY
back cover: Kermit & Piggy photographed by TONY SEINIGER

covers designed by MICHAEL K. FRITH

The MUPPET MOVIE

book adaptation by
STEVEN CRIST
from the filmscript by
JERRY JUHL & JACK BURNS

songs by
PAUL WILLIAMS & KENNY ASCHER

book designed by
IAN SUMMERS & SALLY BASS

A MUPPET PRESS BOOK
from
FONTANA BOOKS

A Henson Organization Publishing Production

AN ORIGINAL FONTANA BOOK
from the MUPPET PRESS

© Henson Associates, Inc. 1979

Printing History:
First Printing: September, 1979

L.C.C. 79-88810

ISBN 0 00 671657 1

First issued in Great Britain by Fontana Books in 1979

Still Photographers: Marcia Reed, Sidney Baldwin and John Shannon
*Miss Piggy in Hollywood: Nancy Moran
Special Thanks to: Ian Ballantine, Dorothy Dodnick,
             Jerry Houle and Leigh Cloniger

Lyrics used by permission of Welbeck Music Corp.
Original soundtrack records and tape available from
Atlantic Records (U.S. and Canada) and CBS Records outside North America.

*MUPPETS, THE MUPPET MOVIE and all character names are trademarks of
Henson Associates, Inc.

PRINTED IN THE UNITED STATES OF AMERICA
by W. A. Krueger Company

0 9 8 7 6 5 4 3 2 1

Dedicated to the memory and magic of Edgar Bergen.

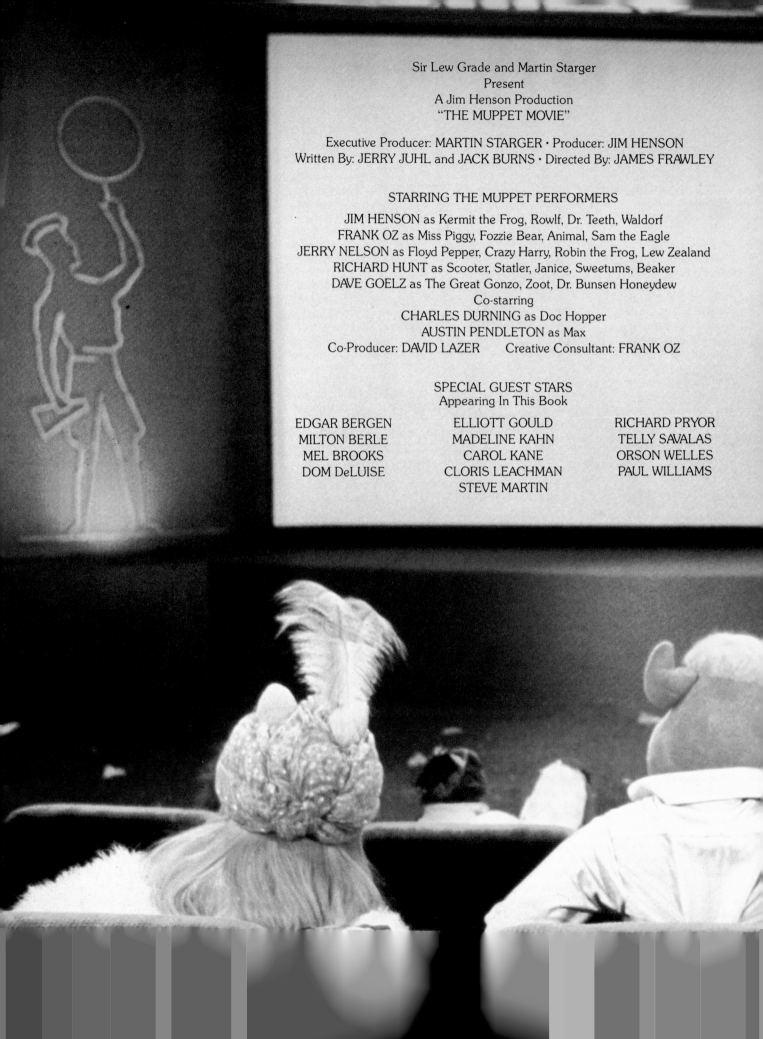

Sir Lew Grade and Martin Starger
Present
A Jim Henson Production
"THE MUPPET MOVIE"

Executive Producer: MARTIN STARGER · Producer: JIM HENSON
Written By: JERRY JUHL and JACK BURNS · Directed By: JAMES FRAWLEY

STARRING THE MUPPET PERFORMERS

JIM HENSON as Kermit the Frog, Rowlf, Dr. Teeth, Waldorf
FRANK OZ as Miss Piggy, Fozzie Bear, Animal, Sam the Eagle
JERRY NELSON as Floyd Pepper, Crazy Harry, Robin the Frog, Lew Zealand
RICHARD HUNT as Scooter, Statler, Janice, Sweetums, Beaker
DAVE GOELZ as The Great Gonzo, Zoot, Dr. Bunsen Honeydew
Co-starring
CHARLES DURNING as Doc Hopper
AUSTIN PENDLETON as Max
Co-Producer: DAVID LAZER   Creative Consultant: FRANK OZ

SPECIAL GUEST STARS
Appearing In This Book

EDGAR BERGEN	ELLIOTT GOULD	RICHARD PRYOR
MILTON BERLE	MADELINE KAHN	TELLY SAVALAS
MEL BROOKS	CAROL KANE	ORSON WELLES
DOM DeLUISE	CLORIS LEACHMAN	PAUL WILLIAMS
	STEVE MARTIN	

with MUPPET PERFORMERS

STEVE WHITMIRE	MICHAEL DAVIS
KATHRYN MULLEN	BUZ SURACI
BOB PAYNE	TONY BASILICATO
EREN OZKER	ADAM HUNT
CAROLY WILCOX	and
OLGA FELGEMACHER	CARROLL SPINNEY
BRUCE SCHWARTZ	as Big Bird

MUPPET DESIGNERS

CAROLY WILCOX	SHERRY AMOTT
MARI KAESTLE	WENDY MIDENER
DAVE GOELZ	JANET LERMAN-GRAFF
KATHRYN MULLEN	BONNIE ERICKSON
ED CHRISTIE	DON SAHLIN
LARRY JAMESON	and
FAZ FAZAKAS	AMY VAN GILDER
KERMIT LOVE	

Muppet Design Consultant: MICHAEL K. FRITH
Muppet Costume Designer: CALISTA HENDRICKSON
Muppet Production Coordinator: LYNN M. KLUGMAN
Distributed By Associated Film Distribution (AFD)

"Gee, Uncle Kermit, is this the true story
of how the Muppets got together?"

"Well, Robin, it's the sort-of-the-way-it-might-
have-happened...I think...true story...."

CHAPTER 1

Deep in the swamp, sun broke through the mist that hung lightly about the ancient cypress trees. There, on his favorite log, sat Kermit the Frog, dreamily strumming his banjo and humming to himself. A beam of sunlight danced across the water and caught on a swirl of mist, forming a hazy rainbow of light around him. Kermit was in a thoughtful mood that morning. He watched a dragonfly dart by, its wings shimmering as it flashed through the rainbow and disappeared into the mist. What did it find there, Kermit wondered, what was there on the rainbow's other side? As he studied the softly changing colors, Kermit's quiet hum turned into a little rainbow song.

Why are there so many
Songs about rainbows,
And what's on the other side?
Rainbows are visions,
But only illusions,
And rainbows have nothing to hide...
So we've been told and
Some choose to believe it,
I know they're wrong wait and see.
Someday we'll find it,
The rainbow connection...
The lovers, the dreamers, and me.

Who said that every wish
Would be heard and answered
When wished on the morning star?

Somebody thought of it
And someone believed it,
Look what we've done so far.
What's so amazing
That keeps us stargazing,
And what do we think we might see?
Someday we'll find it,
The rainbow connection,
The lovers, the dreamers, and me.

All of us under its spell
We know that it's probably magic....

Have you been half asleep,
And have you heard voices?
I've heard them calling my name.
Is this the sweet sound
That calls the young sailors?
The voice might be one and the same.
I've heard it too many times to ignore it,
It's something that I'm supposed to be.
Someday we'll find it,
The rainbow connection,
The lovers, the dreamers, and me.

"WHY ARE THERE SO MANY SONGS ABOUT RAINBOWS..."

The sound of Kermit's banjo faded, and the swamp was silent. Kermit looked around. He loved the old swamp. He had always lived here. Why did he sometimes feel this strange urge to leave this home of his, to search for something different? He was safe here. Out there it was a big world, and... "Help!" A voice echoed through the cypress. "Help! Help!" The voice was coming nearer. But Kermit was lost in thought. What would he *do* if he left the swamp? Maybe, he thought, I could sing my songs for people. Then he thought again: a lover and a dreamer he might be, but who wants a singing frog?"

"HELP! I *REALLY* MEAN HELP!"

There was a frantic splashing and into Kermit's clearing careened a rowboat, a desperate-looking fisherman inexpertly thrashing at the oars.

Kermit could see that this was no garden variety fisherman—more the department store variety. His authentic outdoor-type fisherman's outfit looked as though he'd just taken the price tags off it, and the diamond on his pinkie ring was big enough to hold a hockey game on. The fisherman spotted Kermit.

"Hey, you!" he shouted rudely. "I'm lost! I gotta get outta this swamp!"

"Uh, excuse me a moment," replied Kermit politely. He took aim, calculated airspeed and wind drift and—ZAP!—out shot his tongue as another dragonfly flashed past.

"Darn!" muttered Kermit. "Missed! The tongue is always the first thing to go on a frog."

"Hey, listen," interrupted the fisherman impatiently, "I gotta get outta here! I got a plane to catch."

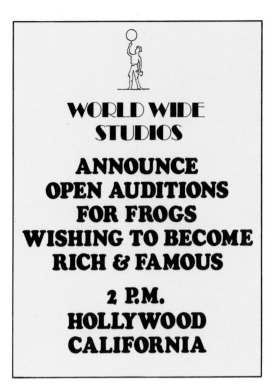

"With that tongue?" mused Kermit. "Forget it!" Kermit thought that was a pretty good line, but the fisherman didn't bite. "But seriously," he hurried on, "there's a boat dock a bit downstream. Just be careful of the alligators."

Funny how that seemed to upset the fisherman.

"Ai-yi-yi! Alligators? We don't have alligators where I come from." He looked around for alligators and, seeing none, continued more confidently. "You see," he looked at Kermit proudly, "I just winged in from Hollywood!"

"No kidding?" Kermit was impressed. "Hollywood, huh?"

"That's right, kid," said the fisherman dramatically. "Hollywood! The Dream Factory! The Magic Store!" He pulled out a copy of *Variety* magazine. "In fact, there's an ad in here you should take a look at."

Kermit read the notice to himself and shook his head. "Oh, well thanks anyway, but I'm pretty happy where I am. I think."

"I'd think about it some more if I were you," the fisherman said. "You got talent, kid! I mean, singing and dancing and telling jokes...you could make millions of people happy."

"What?" Kermit was startled. A *frog* making millions of people happy? Was that possible? A thousand thoughts hopped through Kermit's head, but the fisherman was already rowing away downstream. "If you do come west, frog, look me up," he called. "I'm Bernie the Agent."

"Okay, Bernie the Agent," Kermit yelled back. "By the way, I'd like you to meet Arnie the Alligator."

"Help!" The fisherman was busy breaking the all-time swamp-rowing speed record. "Help! Help, help, help!"

Kermit looked after him for a minute, then picked up his banjo and strummed it softly. "Millions of people happy? Gee, I wonder..."

The next morning Kermit was up with the dawn. If he was going to make that audition, he'd better get on his way. He wrapped his few belongings in a large red bandana, slung his banjo over his shoulder, took one last look at the old swamp, pointed the front wheel of his bicycle in the direction of Hollywood and pedaled off. The time had come to give his dream a chance.

CHAPTER 2

For some time Kermit's bicycle bumped along quiet country roads, then gradually the way became wider and smoother and houses began to dot the countryside. So this was the outside world. Kermit stared in fascination at the brightly painted roadside signs: MOTEL-TV-SWIMMING POOL! read one. BEST BURGERS IN THE SOUTH! said another. And there was one just being put up: COMING SOON—ANOTHER DOC HOPPER'S FRENCH FRIED FROGS' LEGS… Kermit was stunned. Frogs' legs? Aack! He didn't even see the steamroller… "Look out!" yelled a man working on the sign.

With a sickening crunch the steamroller rumbled over Kermit's bicycle, leaving it crushed in the pavement. And what of its rider? "Whew," gasped Kermit, sitting high atop the steamroller, "it's a good thing us frogs know how to hop. Otherwise I'd be—" he looked back at his crumpled bike, "gone with the Schwinn!"

But the man painting the sign wasn't looking at the bicycle. He was looking at Kermit the Frog… and licking his lips.

Well, Kermit thought, there goes my transportation. Now how was he going to get to Hollywood? There wasn't much choice. And so, with a sigh, he set off down the road, putting one flipper in front of the other.

By nightfall Kermit found himself in the seedy part of a strange town far from the familiar and friendly surroundings of the swamp. He was flipper-weary and famished. Someday he might make millions of people happy, but right now all he cared about was making one frog a little less miserable. He decided to get some dinner.

Down the street he saw a tacky sign blinking: THE EL SLEEZO CAFE, it read. The paint was peeling off the building and garbage was heaped high around the entrance. From inside came the sound of shouts and breaking glass.

"The El Sleezo, huh?" Kermit winced. "Well, a frog's gotta eat," and squaring his little green shoulders, he marched toward the door.

At that moment another customer left rather quickly.

With a groan, the man pulled himself out of a heap of garbage cans. Kermit swallowed nervously. "Uh, rough place, huh?"

"This place?" growled the man. "Yucch! This is the *toughest*... the *meanest*... the *filthiest* pesthole on the face of the earth."

"Why not complain to the owner?" Kermit suggested.

"I *am* the owner," snarled the owner. He shoved his hat over his ears and his hands into his pockets and stumbled off into the night.

"Well," gulped Kermit, "l-like I said, a f-frog's gotta eat," and he pushed his trembling green knees through the swinging doors of the El Sleezo Cafe.

Kermit the Frog blinked his eyes several times at the scene before him. The El Sleezo looked like a combination of every crummy joint in every crummy movie Kermit had ever seen. The room was filled with a heady cloud of cheap perfume and cheaper beer and an unsavory bunch of patrons who looked like they'd kill their own grandmothers for five bucks—and yours for nothing. The swamp could get a little ripe sometimes, but this...There was the sound of a scuffle in the balcony above, and with a splintering crash a cowboy toppled through the railing and plummeted to the floor, narrowly missing the terrified frog. Kermit hurried to the bar and tried to blend in quietly. The woman next to him leaned over and whispered in his ear.

"Hello, sailor," she cooed, "buy me a drink?"

"I'm not a sailor, I'm a frog," the baffled frog replied.

"Cut the small talk and buy me a drink!"

"Hey, you!" one of the meanest-looking tough guys Kermit had ever seen growled at him. "Are you making a pass at my girl?"

"N-n-no, sir," trembled Kermit.

"Yes, he was," the woman insisted. "He touched me!"

"Yecch!" yelled the man. "Go wash! You'll get warts!" The woman ran off. Now there's nothing that makes a frog mad quicker than a wart joke. "That's a myth," Kermit informed the man, indignantly.

"Yeth, and she's *my* mith!" The man looked like he was ready to use Kermit's face to mop up the floor. Kermit looked wildly around for an escape. At that moment the sound of an alarm clock cut through the racket, and everyone's attention turned to the piano player in the corner, who, having awakened with a startled jerk, was now swatting at the clock.

"Showtime!" he croaked, thumping out some tinny chords on the broken-down piano. "It's showtime at the ol' El Sleezo!"

That was a relief! Kermit turned to watch the show, while the rest of the crowd settled into what seats were available—and some that weren't.

"And now," shouted the piano player, "here, filling in for the vacationing El-Sleezo Cuties…" the angry murmur grew louder—it was hard to believe, but the crowd was growing uglier by the minute — "…is that madcap master of merciless mirth, the funny…the furry….the fabulous…Fozzie Bear!"

"Ta-daaaah!" clunked the piano. From behind the curtain, out sprang a bear wearing a brown hat, a polka dot tie, and a false nose and glasses. He immediately whipped off the false nose and glasses to reveal…. another false nose and glasses. This was a stand-up bear who would do *anything* for a laugh.

"Hiya! Hiya! Hiya!"
"This is Fozzie Bear!
I'll tell you jokes
both old and rare!"

*Waldorf: Did he say his jokes
were rare?
Statler: Yeah. That's because
they're not well done!
Both: Ho, ho! Heh! Urf, urf!*

"Well, um, starting off with a bang," Fozzie struggled on. "Say! Didja hear the one about the sailor who was so incredibly fat that...."

Fozzie's words died on his lips. Slowly, from the audience a sailor was rising who must have weighed 400 pounds before breakfast. In one meaty fist he wielded a broken beer bottle.

"He-he was so fat," the bear was stammering weakly, "that everyone loved him and—oh, help!"

Kermit sadly shook his head. Now the audience was encouraging Fozzie with a cascade of vegetables.

Kermit couldn't sit by any longer. This was a nice guy just trying to make people laugh, make them happy, and here he was being bombarded by beets. It was time to act! Kermit hopped on to the stage and yelled into Fozzie's ear.

"C'mon. Dance!"

"Wha'?" replied the startled bear. "Oh! Yessir!"

To the sound of the tinny piano, the two stumbled into a soft-shoe shuffle, unaware that through the window of the El Sleezo Cafe two sinister sets of eyes were greedily staring at the nimble legs of Kermit the Frog.

Had Kermit seen the two men crouched outside the window, he might have recognized one as the man at work that morning on the ghastly billboard for Doc Hopper's French Fried Frogs' Legs. And the other? Had Kermit had time to study the face on the billboard, he might have recognized…Doc Hopper himself! As he peered through the window, Hopper's beady eyes glistened in his round, perspiring face. Those were million-dollar legs!

For a moment the sight of a frog and a bear doing a dance number was enough to quiet the crowd. But the novelty soon wore thin and the angry shouts rose to a roar.

"Let's get 'em!"

The entire mob rushed the stage, kicking and fighting to see who could get at Kermit and Fozzie.

AR-GA-Raga-ORK!

CRASH!

LOOK OUT!

CRUNCH!

EEEYOW!

EEEOW!

OUCH!

TAKE THAT!

ARRGH!

ARRGH!

CRASH!

WHY YOU...

OUCH!

BASH!

BASH!

CRUNCH!

BRE-AK!

HIT!

And so forth.

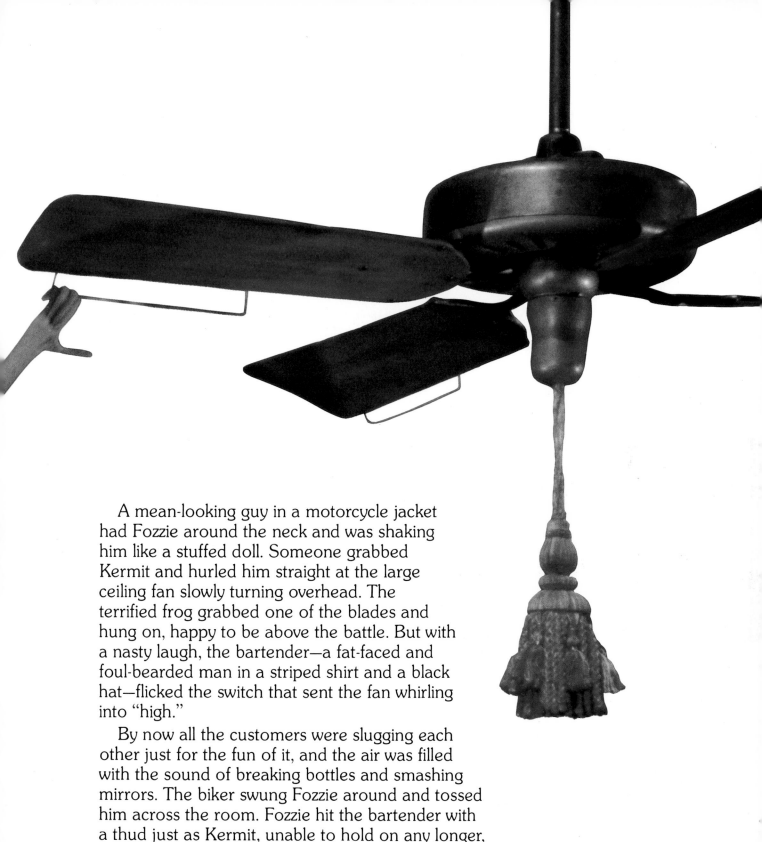

A mean-looking guy in a motorcycle jacket had Fozzie around the neck and was shaking him like a stuffed doll. Someone grabbed Kermit and hurled him straight at the large ceiling fan slowly turning overhead. The terrified frog grabbed one of the blades and hung on, happy to be above the battle. But with a nasty laugh, the bartender—a fat-faced and foul-bearded man in a striped shirt and a black hat—flicked the switch that sent the fan whirling into "high."

By now all the customers were slugging each other just for the fun of it, and the air was filled with the sound of breaking bottles and smashing mirrors. The biker swung Fozzie around and tossed him across the room. Fozzie hit the bartender with a thud just as Kermit, unable to hold on any longer, flew off the fan and into the piano. The piano player, again jolted from his sleep, sat bolt upright and struck another resounding "Ta-daaah!"

The puzzled mob paused for a moment in its mayhem, and Fozzie, dressed in a black hat, striped shirt, and foul beard, popped up from behind the bar.

"Okay, everybody," announced the Bear, "drinks are on the house!"

"Hooray!" shouted the patrons, and to the amazement of Kermit the Frog they abandoned their mauling and mangling and dashed out of the bar.

"Drinks on the house?" asked the baffled frog.

"Works every time," replied the self-satisfied bear.

"DRINKS ARE ON THE HOUSE!"

"OK. Where's the drinks?"

"Make mine sarsaparilla!"

"Is this some kind of joke?"

Kermit looked curiously at Fozzie. They'd only known each other for ten minutes, but there was something about this bear… "Look," Kermit said quickly. "I'm on my way to Hollywood. World Wide Studios is holding auditions for frogs in a few days. If they need frogs, they must need bears. Want to join me?"

Fozzie was amazed. "Hollywood? It's always been my dream! My car's outside."

The two new friends hurried out to Fozzie's car.
"Hey, where'd you get this Studebaker, Fozzie?"
"My uncle left it to me."
"Is he dead?"
"No, hibernating."
Kermit gave Fozzie a strange look and hopped into the Studebaker. With a terrible crunch of grinding gears, Fozzie drove off into the night.
"Say," mused Kermit, after a while, "if we're going to Hollywood together, how about you and me putting together an act? A little song and dance team?"
"Nope, sorry, Kermit," said Fozzie firmly, "I work alone."
Kermit shrugged his shoulders. Oh well, he thought, I guess everyone's entitled to his own dreams. There was a long silence as the two sat lost in thought. "OK," said Fozzie suddenly, "you talked me into it! We'll be a team."
As the new team shook hands and dreamed of overnight success and making millions of people happy, they were not aware that something was following them—a long, black limousine that slunk after them like a deadly panther with two sets of beady sinister eyes.

CHAPTER 3

Fozzie slammed on the brakes and screeched to a stop. A sawhorse loomed ahead of them in the middle of the road.

"What the hey…?" Kermit began.

The black limousine pulled swiftly up beside them, a door slammed and over to Kermit's window waddled Doc Hopper.

"Well, howdy there, Mr. Frog," said the fat man with an unctuous grin, "I'm a businessman with a proposition. There's five hundred big ones in it for you. Step outside and let me show ya what I mean." He fanned out five crisp hundred dollar bills. Slowly the puzzled frog and bear climbed out of their car.

Smiling proudly, Hopper pointed toward a store window filled with television sets. He pulled a remote-control device out of his pocket, aimed it at the window, and clicked it once. Immediately the television screens sprang to life. "Watch this!" he grinned.

COMMERCIAL

"Hi! I'm Doc Hopper,
invitin' you to hop on down
and get some Hopper's French
Fried Frogs' Legs right here
at the Sign of the Bright Green Legs.

"Frogs' legs, frogs' legs,
frogs' legs so fine!
Hopper's is the place you should dine.
There's cheese legs, bacon legs,
chile legs too,
French fried frogs' legs and barbecue!

"If you want just a snack,
Then here is the one,
A frog leg burger on a bright green bun.

"So like we say down at
Doc Hopper's,
Hop on down . . . we hop that
you do!"

Kermit was horrified. "That's the most appalling, disgusting, revolting thing I've ever seen!" he yelled.

"I know," drawled Doc with a hearty smile. "I'm a great businessman and a sweet fella. I do, however, make a terrible frog. You, on the other hand, would make a *terrific* frog."

"You *are* very likable, Kermit," said Fozzie cheerfully.

"The bear's right," oozed Doc. "*You,* my likable little friend, are going to do all our television commercials."

Kermit blanched. "Me?"

"That's right," said Doc excitedly. "*You!* Singin' and dancin' your way into millions of living rooms all across the country. What do you say?"

Kermit couldn't believe this. Sure, he wanted to sing and dance for millions of people, but not like this, not to sell them…*frogs' legs!*

"No way," snapped Kermit, and headed for the car. Fozzie was puzzled. Here was a chance to be in Show Business—and five hundred dollars…? He sidled up to Hopper. "Would you consider a bear in a frog suit…?"

"Fozzie!" yelled Kermit from the car.

"Yessir!" said the bear, and hopped in beside him. Off down the road rattled the Studebaker.

Hopper turned to Max. "Follow that frog!" he screamed.

Max dutifully jumped in the limousine, gunned the accelerator, and roared after Kermit and Fozzie.

"I knew you'd like the frog, boss, isn't he terrific? Isn't he?…Boss?"

Max stopped the car, turned around, and looked into the back seat. There was no sign of Doc! Then through the rear window Max saw Doc running after the limousine, still screaming. Max couldn't make out what he was saying, but it didn't sound too complimentary.

Movin' right along in search of
good times and good news,
With good friends you can't lose,
this could become a habit.

Movin' right along
We'll learn to share the load,
We don't need a map to keep this
show on the road.

Movin' right along
Hey L.A. where've you gone?
Send someone to fetch us
we're in Saskatchewan!

We'll buy sandals very comfy, all
hand-tooled leather,
Unusual weather,
Mid-July and it's still snowin'?

Opportunity knocks but once,
*   let's reach out and grab it,*
With luck of foot
*   from lucky rabbit!*

Movin' right along
*   Footloose and fancy free,*
Gettin' there is half the fun, come
*   share it with me.*

Movin' right along we found a life
*   on the highway,*
And your way is my way,
*   So trust my navigation.*

California here we come
*   To pie in the sky land,*
Palm trees and warm sand,
*   Tho' sadly we just left Rhode Island.*

Movin' right along
*   You take it, you know best…*
Plus I've never seen the sun
*   come up in the west!*

Movin' right along
*   We're truly birds of a feather,*
We're in this together,
*   And you know where you're goin'.*

Movin' right along,
*   Hurray two signs of men:*
"Welcome" on the same post
*   that says "Come back again!"*

Movin' right along
*   This map ain't really clear,*
But goin' nowhere fast paid off—
*   We're finally here!*

It was a glorious morning, so fresh and full of
promise that Kermit and Fozzie hardly felt that
they'd been driving all night. Kermit, whistling and
plinking his banjo, gazed out the window at the
passing farms and billboards. Suddenly he let out
a shriek. Fozzie slammed on the brakes. Before
them, stood a sign for Doc Hopper's French
Fried Frogs' Legs. But instead of the grinning
visage of Doc Hopper in the middle of the sign,
there, crude but unmistakable, was the face of
Kermit the Frog. And the paint was still wet.

Kermit sat stunned, hardly noticing Doc
running out from behind the billboard. He was
followed by Max, wearing overalls, covered with
green paint, and grinning.

"You get the picture, boy?" crowed Doc
delightedly. "See what I mean? *Kermit the
Frog—symbol of Doc Hopper's French Fried
Frogs' Legs!*"

Kermit's eyes glazed over. "All I can see," he
croaked, "is millions of frogs on tiny crutches."

Max was startled. "Crutches...?" He turned to Doc.

"Listen, boy," growled Doc, ignoring Max,
"we'll put up so many billboards, why, your face
will be a household word!"

"Crutches...?" Max's eyes were wide.

"Shut up, Max," snapped Doc. He turned to Kermit with a huge grin. "Look, frog, don't you want to become rich and famous?"

"Not working for *you* I don't." Kermit turned to Fozzie. "Let's get out of here." Fozzie slammed into gear and the Studebaker lurched off, leaving the Frog Leg King in a cloud of dust. Hopper shook his fist after the departing car.

"I've done my best with that frog," growled Doc, spitting out the dust, "now it's time to do my worst! Come on Max."

But Max was standing completely still, apparently transfixed. Then, slowly, he drew himself up, threw back his head, and looked Doc in the eye. "You go ahead, Doc," he said quietly but firmly. "I'm through. The frog is right. You're asking him to do something terrible. I...I can't be part of it." Max was growing bolder with each word. His voice rose. "It's a moral decision! And I'll stand by it!!"

Doc studied his young assistant for a moment, then said softly, "I'll double your percentage."

Max dove for the driver's seat. "Let's go!" he yelled.

Safely ahead of them, Kermit and Fozzie were moving right along the highway, but the morning's good feeling was gone. They were exhausted.

"I think we lost them, Kermit."

Kermit was getting a permanent crick in his neck from looking back over his shoulder. "OK, I guess we're safe. Let's pull over and rest for a minute."

Fozzie slowed the car and stopped under a huge shady tree. They were in an abandoned country churchyard, and next to them stood a little white clapboard church with a stubby bell tower. It was as peaceful a place as one could hope for.

"Feels like we've been driving for days," sighed Kermit wearily.

"Funny, I'm wide awake," yawned Fozzie.

In a moment the two had fallen into a deep and welcome sleep.

CHAPTER 4

It was the loudest pounding noise Kermit or Fozzie had ever heard. They bolted upright in their seats, startled and terrified. What was going on? As their heads cleared, they realized that what they were hearing was the thunderous sound of a rock and roll band, and it was coming from inside the church. Kermit and Fozzie knew there was no hope of getting any more sleep, so they climbed out of the car to investigate.

Together the two friends walked nervously to the front door and peered in.

Inside, the church had been stripped of everything except a few bright stained-glass windows, some pews and an old pipe organ. The wild music was being made by five of the wildest musicians Kermit had ever seen.

The musicians seemed delighted to see them. "Hey, hey," rasped the organist to his cohorts, "our gentle morning melodies have attracted wandering admirers." There could be no doubt—this dude was hip.

Kermit and Fozzie picked their way through the heavy undergrowth of electrical cords and cables and approached the band. "Who are you guys?" ventured the shorter and greener of the two.

"We," said the jive bassist, "am-is-are-be they whom are known as The Electric Mayhem. The cat on the organ is Doctor Teeth. Me, I'm Floyd. Meet Janice, lead guitar, and that's Zoot—he plays sax."

"Uh…yeah, I'm Sax and I play zoot."

"Right," continued Floyd. "Up there is Scooter—he's our man with the van—and this here is Animal. He beats drum."

"Beat drum!" bellowed Animal.

"See, we're fixing up this church here," explained Scooter enthusiastically.

"It's going to be a coffee house," added Janice. "You know, good music and organic refreshment?"

"Yeah, it'll be so fine and mellow and laid back," cooed Doctor Teeth, "…and profitable."

"But tell us," Floyd asked the visitors, "what brings you two gentlemen here?" Fozzie liked the sound of that; he'd never been called a gentleman before, certainly not back at the El Sleezo.

"Well, heyyy! It's a great story! You see, Kermit here was living in a swamp and then this fisherman—"

"Fozzie, you can't tell the story all over again. You'll bore the people reading this book."

Fozzie was perplexed. "But the band here wants to know, Kermit."

"Here, let them read the script while we get some sleep."

"Oh, yessir!" Fozzie handed the script to Doctor Teeth, and he and Kermit curled up on a pew and quickly fell asleep.

"Let's see, here we go," said the Doctor. "Scene One—Exterior—Swamp—Day: Sun breaks through the mist that hangs lightly about the ancient cypress trees…"

"...'But the band here wants to know, Kermit.' 'Here, let them read the script while we get some sleep.'" Doctor Teeth put down the script and sat for a moment in silence. "That, my friends," he said, "is a very heavy duty story."

"Sure is," said Floyd. "Man, he's just got to keep his little froggy self away from this Hopper dude!"

"Oooh, like, what can we do to help them?" Janice looked at the frog and bear asleep on the pew.

Doctor Teeth thought hard for a
minute then his eye fell on Scooter's
pots of paint. Slowly he smiled from
tooth to tooth, no mean feat for him.
    "Grab those paint pots and make
tracks for that Studebaker," he rasped.
"I think I got an idea."

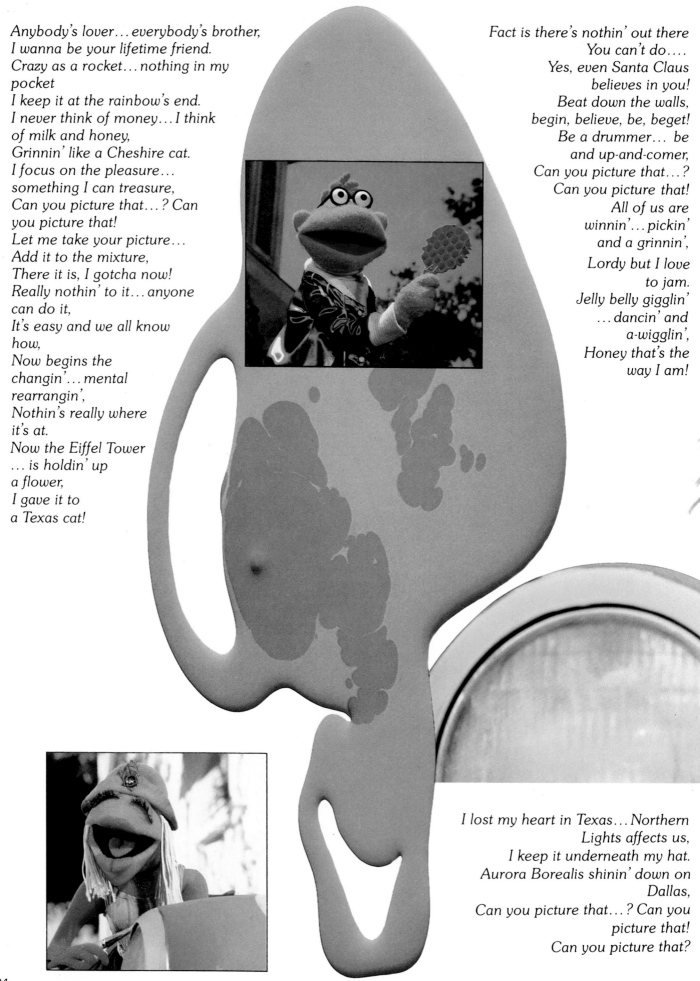

Anybody's lover…everybody's brother,
I wanna be your lifetime friend.
Crazy as a rocket…nothing in my pocket
I keep it at the rainbow's end.
I never think of money…I think of milk and honey,
Grinnin' like a Cheshire cat.
I focus on the pleasure…something I can treasure,
Can you picture that…? Can you picture that!
Let me take your picture…
Add it to the mixture,
There it is, I gotcha now!
Really nothin' to it…anyone can do it,
It's easy and we all know how,
Now begins the changin'…mental rearrangin',
Nothin's really where it's at.
Now the Eiffel Tower
…is holdin' up
a flower,
I gave it to
a Texas cat!

Fact is there's nothin' out there
You can't do….
Yes, even Santa Claus
believes in you!
Beat down the walls,
begin, believe, be, beget!
Be a drummer… be
and up-and-comer,
Can you picture that…?
Can you picture that!
All of us are
winnin'…pickin'
and a grinnin',
Lordy but I love
to jam.
Jelly belly gigglin'
…dancin' and
a-wigglin',
Honey that's the
way I am!

I lost my heart in Texas…Northern
Lights affects us,
I keep it underneath my hat.
Aurora Borealis shinin' down on
Dallas,
Can you picture that…? Can you
picture that!
Can you picture that?

Dr. Teeth put down his paintbrush and chuckled. "That does it," he smiled. "Doc Hopper will never recognize them now."

The last time that Kermit and Fozzie had awakened, they couldn't believe their ears. This time, they couldn't believe their eyes. There stood Fozzie's Studebaker, freshly painted in a dizzying, dazzling display of psychedelic designs. "I don't know how to thank you," Fozzie gasped in awe.

"I don't know *why* to thank you," said Kermit a bit skeptically.

"It was our pleasure, greenstuff," said Floyd proudly.

"Heyyyy," said Fozzie, struck with a brainstorm, "why don't you guys come to Hollywood with us?"

"Can't, baby," chuckled the toothy doctor. "But when you get rich and famous, maybe we'll show up and exploit your wealth."

Reluctantly, Kermit and Fozzie said good-bye to the Mayhem, and hit the road once more. They didn't know that about a mile up that road there was parked a black limousine, its engines idling, its occupants both dreaming of one thing—money.

"Double my percentage!" Max was murmuring to himself. "Lemme see…if my share of the profits is one-fifth of one percent, then if I double that—" he paused uncertainly "—maybe I'll hire an accountant."

"Max," mused Doc, "that frog is worth a million bucks!"

"How much is my share of a million?" Max was excited.

"Oh, it could easily come to…one, maybe two hundred. Look, Max, forget the money. Just find me a frog and a bear in a tan Studebaker."

Max glanced at an unusual car that was passing them, then shook his head. "Sorry, Doc," he said, "all I see is a frog and a bear in a rainbow-colored Studebaker."

"Too bad," growled Doc. "*What?* After them!"

Fozzie saw the limo in the rearview mirror. He gunned the car around a tight bend in the road. Just ahead, Kermit saw a big billboard advertising a soft drink.

"AFTER THEM!"

"QUICK, FOZZIE! PULL OVER THERE!"

Fozzie swerved off the road and up a grassy embankment, lurching to a stop in front of the billboard just as Doc and Max sped by.

"They've disappeared," said Max.

"Must've missed 'em," Doc said unhappily. "Turn around."

Max screeched to a stop, switched off the engine, and turned to face Doc with a smile.

Doc stared at Max in disbelief.

"No," he whispered furiously. "The *car*, Max. Turn the *car* around!"

CHAPTER 5

About a mile ahead of Fozzie and Kermit, a battered old panel truck was bumping its way in their direction. On its side was painted in large erratic lettering, "Gonzo the Great—Plumbing Artiste." Behind the wheel sat Gonzo the Great himself, and beside him was a large, white and very beautiful chicken.

"You know, Camilla," the plumbing artiste was saying to the chicken, "great plumbers are born, not made. I am a prince of the plunger, fair maiden." He studied Camilla to see what kind of impression he was making. Camilla let out a terrified squawk. Headed straight down the highway toward them, was a rainbow-colored Studebaker.

"Fozzie, LOOK OUT!" screamed Kermit. The old panel truck was coming right at them. "OH NO!" Kermit's life flashed before his eyes. The swamp…? Hollywood…? Was this the end of his dream?

"LOOK OUT!"

"LOOK OUT!" Fozzie hit the brakes and swerved hard, but it was too late. Kermit covered his face with his hands. He heard a horrible crunching of metal and …

"What the hey?" Kermit shook his head and looked around. The Studebaker had come to a stop. There was no sign of the truck.

Then, to their astonishment, a peculiar head with an enormous curved beak appeared upside down in the windshield.

"Hi!" said Gonzo brightly.

Kermit got out of the car and stared open-mouthed at the sight that met his eyes. The plumbing truck had done a complete flip and landed nearly on top of the Studebaker, where it now seemed permanently stuck.

Gonzo and Camilla climbed into the back seat of the Studebaker, where the Prince of the Plunger proceeded to hop furiously up and down.

"What are you doing *that* for?" asked the puzzled frog.

"Because I'm hopping mad!" retorted the plumber. Kermit, always on the lookout for humor, smiled appreciatively.

"Heyyyy," suggested Fozzie, "seeing as how we've only got one car left, why don't you guys join us on our trip?"

"Sure," added Kermit, "you look like our kind of … whatever you are." He was pretty sure that Camilla was a chicken, but it was hard to tell about Gonzo.

"Where are you going?" asked Gonzo.

"We're following our dream!" said Fozzie grandly.

BOMBAY

"Really? Wow, I have a dream, too," said Gonzo excitedly, "it's.... but," his voice dropped to a shy whisper, "you'll think it's dumb." "No, we won't," Kermit said. "Well," said Gonzo, eagerly, "I want to go to Bombay, India, and become a *movie star!!*" There was a moment of stunned silence, finally broken by Fozzie. "You don't go to *India* to become a movie star," he explained patiently. "You go to *Hollywood.*" "Oh, sure," replied the exasperated Gonzo, "if you want to do it the easy way." Kermit and Fozzie exchanged a quick look. "Uh-oh," whispered Fozzie, "we've picked up a weirdo."

The road they were driving on finally led to a small town, and there before them loomed a large sign, MAD MAN MOONEY'S HUBCAP HEAVEN. It was a used car lot. They turned into the lot just as their bizarre car wheezed its last. Out sprang the Mad Man himself.

"Aha, my friends, this is your lucky day," announced Mooney.

"It is?" Fozzie was intrigued.

"That's right, Mister Bear. You, for example, are driving the wrong car."

"I am?" Fozzie was puzzled.

"That's right, my friend, and for only two thousand dollars—minus, of course, the generous twelve dollar trade-in on your old…*vehicle*—I can give you *this*!" The Mad Man proudly patted a rusty Volkswagen, whose left fender promptly fell to the ground with a crash. Mooney feigned outrage.

"Hey, what's this pile of junk doing out here?" he yelled to someone sitting back in the office. "Get rid of this heap!" He turned back to Fozzie. "Heh-heh, just kidding."

From the office, out ran Mooney's assistant, your typical eight-foot-tall, fur-covered car lot worker. "Get that piece of trash out of here, Sweetums, and step on it!" snapped Mooney.

Sweetums picked up the car as if it were a wheelbarrow and rolled it away, grinning to himself and lazily shooing off a fly that buzzed around his furry head.

**The Madman sez:
"The Price you see
is the Price you pay!"**

The Mad Man proceeded to show them one junky car after another, each more outrageously priced than the one before it.

"You," he was saying to Kermit, "I see in a swamp buggy. Now right here I've got…"

Sweetums trotted back from disposing of the Volkswagen. He seemed particularly interested in what was going on, and Kermit noticed that every time the Mad Man made a preposterous offer, Sweetums would shake his head.

Finally, Mooney came to a nifty little wood-paneled station wagon, and Sweetums began jumping excitedly up and down. It was indeed the perfect car, but Kermit shook his head sadly at the pricetag. They could never afford $1195.

Just then the fly that had been pestering Sweetums buzzed past the little station wagon, and taking deadly aim, the monster gave it a swat. "Hey! We'll take that one!" Kermit yelled excitedly, pointing to the woody. The Mad Man looked around victoriously, then turned a ghastly white as he noticed the pricetag.

"Hey! We'll take that one!"

"So, less our twelve dollar trade-in," Gonzo figured quickly as the Mad Man struggled to regain his breath, "you owe *us* five cents."

Mooney fumbled dazedly for a nickel and looked with disgust at the frog who'd just made the buy of the century. "A frog, a bear, two weird birds…" he muttered, "they have a jailbreak at the zoo?"

Fozzie chuckled wholeheartedly. "You keep that nickel, sir, it's been worth it to me, hearing all your wonderful jokes."

Kermit walked over to Sweetums. The tall fellow still hadn't said a word, but he'd sure arranged a good deal on the car for them. There was something about him…

"Hey, we're going to Hollywood," said Kermit brightly. "You want to come along?"

"What?!" screamed Sweetums. He turned and ran into the office.

Kermit was surprised. "Strange," he said to the others as they got into their new car. "Somehow he seemed like one of us. Oh well, let's go."

Off they drove in their new station wagon, just too soon to see a shaggy former car-salesman's assistant run out of the office with a big valise.

"Hey, wait!" yelled Sweetums, chasing after them. "You're my kind of guys! Wait for me!"

**"Hey wait!
You're my kind of guys!
Wait for me!"**

46

CHAPTER 6

The little station wagon pushed steadily westward. The countryside was beautiful, there was no sign of Doc Hopper, and Kermit was beginning to relax again. Down the highway he could see a cluster of tents, some gaily painted booths and rows of flapping flags shining in the Midwest sunshine. It was a county fair.

"Hey, Fozzie. Let's stop and take a look."

The four tumbled out of the car and were quickly swept up in the crowd that was converging on the main tent. "Step right up, folks!" boomed a voice over the loudspeakers. "Step right up and meet the most beautiful girls in Bogen County!"

The crowd gathered around expectantly.

"Yes, it's the moment we've all been waiting for," proclaimed the oily master of ceremonies. "The winners of this year's Miss Bogen County Beauty Pageant… Second Runner-up, Miss Debbie Sue Anderson… and First Runner-up, Alma Jane Gitnick!" The girls rushed giggling onto the stage and the M.C. winked broadly. "Boy, we sure grow 'em pretty around here, don't we? Now, before we announce Miss Bogen County herself, I'd like to thank our esteemed judges, Edgar Bergen and Charlie McCarthy!" The judges took a brief bow, and from somewhere off-stage a drumroll began.

"And now," the M.C. was enjoying himself immensely, "the moment you've all been waiting for, America's sweetheart, here she is, the winner…"

"Bergen, you'll never believe who the winner is."

"Now, now Charlie. It's their movie."

"...MISS PIGGY!"

From behind the curtain stepped the new Miss Bogen County, a veritable vision of piggish pulchritude. Full-bodied and golden-tressed, her blue eyes sparkling as brightly as the shimmering rhinestone crown that was placed upon her head, she made her way regally to the awaiting throne. The stage was hers!

The awestruck audience was silent for a moment, then burst into applause and cheers. These were farmers and they knew a beautiful pig when they saw one!

"Ooh, kissy-kissy!" squealed the object of this adulation. "Thank you! Thank you! I'd just like to say that..."

It was like a bolt from the blue. There, on the fringe of the crowd, her eyes had suddenly locked on the handsomest, most glorious creature she had ever seen. Instantly she forgot where she was, who she was. A mighty tidal wave swept over her as she felt herself transported beyond time and space on a surge of pure ecstatic love. True, he was shorter than some and greener than most, but this, she knew, was the man of her dreams, her prince, her destiny. Never before, she thought...never before... and never again...

NEVER BEFORE HAVE
TWO SOULS JOINED
SO FREELY
AND SO FAST,

*For me this is the first time
And the last…*

*Is this an angel's wish for men?
Never before and never again!
And where to find the words
To sing its worth…?*

*This love was bound for heaven
Not for earth,
This love was meant to light the stars…
But when we touched*

We made it ours…
And could they take it back?
Oh no, they wouldn't dare!
Why should they take it back

When there's enough
To share with all the world
And fill the heavens above
With leftover love….

Never before,
A love that just keeps growing
On and on…
To fill each lover's heart

And light the dawn…
Is this an angel's wish for men?
Never before and never again…
Never before and never again!

Kermit the Frog was trying, without being rude, to extricate himself from the passionate embrace of an admittedly glamorous, but rather forceful, lady pig.

"Er, Miss," he stammered, "you seem to have, uh, attached yourself to me."

"Hmmmmmm?" murmured Miss Piggy dreamily. "Ooh! Dear me!" She pulled away, somewhat flustered, but still unable to take her eyes off this magnificent specimen of froghood.

"Uhh, congratulations on winning the beauty contest," offered Kermit.

"Oh, thank you, Frog of my Heart," Piggy sighed. Then, quickly she regained her composure. "Of course, I don't *usually* do anything this...*trivial*. I," she continued a bit haughtily, "am an actress-model."

Fozzie was baffled. He didn't know what was going on here, but he did know there were important matters to attend to. "Hey, Kermit," he interrupted, "I thought we were going to get some ice cream."

"Uh, you guys go ahead," said Kermit in a daze, "we'll be along in a minute."

Piggy sidled up to him as the others left. She was breathing hard. "Just what brings you to town, short-green-and-handsome?"

"We're heading, uh"—something told Kermit that he shouldn't be too specific about their destination "—west." He didn't quite understand what was happening, and he wasn't sure he wanted to. "Hey, listen," he said, changing the subject quickly, "the others have gone for ice cream. Want to come along?"

Miss Piggy's eyes lit up. "Why, I'd LOVE to!" she cried and instantly ran off in another direction. Kermit, now thoroughly confused, shrugged his shoulders and walked toward the ice cream stand.

Gonzo and Camilla, meanwhile, had found their way to the balloon seller. "I'll buy you one, Camilla, but you have to choose the color. Red or green?"

The balloon seller leaned over to Gonzo. "Pssst!… Hey, you," he whispered conspiratorially, "c'mere." Gonzo cocked his head.

"Lemme offer you a word of advice, bud: get her *both* balloons. Why, sometimes," the man continued, looking around and narrowing his *eyes*, "I seen guys buy a whole *bunch* of balloons for their girls. They go ga-ga for it!"

"I'll do it!" said Gonzo impulsively. "What d'you say, Camilla!"

"Ga-ga, ga-ga!" cried Camilla.

"GA-GA, GA-GA!"

Kermit found Fozzie at the ice cream stand. "Hi, Kermit, where's your pig friend?" he asked through a mouthful of honey-mocha. Before Kermit could reply, a pink streak hefting a large lavender vanity case was at his side. "I'm packed!" announced Miss Piggy.

"Uh, so I...see," replied Kermit, afraid to ask what for. "What for?"

"You said I could come with you," she reminded him sweetly.

"F-for ice cream, not to *Hollywood*," cried Kermit desperately. He felt trapped.

"We're going to *Hollywood?*" Miss Piggy's eyes were glazed with joy.

"No—see, when I said—I mean—when you said that—oh, brother..."

There was a terrified squawk from Camilla, and Kermit wheeled around to an incredible sight. The Great Gonzo, plumbing artiste,

was slowly and majestically rising above them, borne aloft by a large bunch of balloons.

Kermit's mind was completely boggled. "What are you *doing?*" he shrieked after the floating Gonzo.

"Oh," he replied, carefully considering the question, "about…seven…knots."

Camilla was still squawking hysterically and pulling at Kermit's arm.

"Don't worry," he reassured her. "Fozzie! Quick! We'll follow him in the car! Let's go!"

Into the car they piled, Fozzie at the wheel, Kermit yelling directions, Piggy next to him, and Camilla wailing in the back seat.

"There he goes, Fozzie, turn left! No, no, the wind's changing, *right!*" Back and forth they careened, so intent on following Gonzo that they didn't notice the big black limousine that had swerved into their path and was following them.

Doc couldn't believe his good luck. "Don't let 'em get away, Max!" he yelled. He slipped two shells into his shotgun and leaned out the window. Ahead of them the station wagon was zigzagging wildly across a field. The limousine bounced after them. A gust of wind caught the Prince of the Plunger and wafted him toward a large and rather ugly billboard advertising AUNT AMY'S CUSTARD PIES. On it was a picture of Aunt Amy herself, holding up one of her wares.

"Okay, Fozzie, left, left! Faster… Good! Now, he's right above us! Left, right… LOOK OUT!"

CRASH! The station wagon ploughed into the billboard.

WHOOSH! The eight-foot-wide banana cream pie flew out of Aunt Amy's hand!

SPLAT! The pie hit the limousine's windshield!

SCREECH! Max slammed on the brakes.

BLAM! Doc jerked forward, accidentally firing his shotgun.

POWPOWPOWPOWPOWPOWPOWPOW!

All but one of Gonzo's balloons burst, popped by the blast from Doc's gun. Down plummeted the brave balloonist, falling, by sheer luck, exactly on top of the station wagon.

"I'm back," Gonzo announced calmly.

CRASH!

WHOOSH!

SPLAT!

SCREECH!

BLAM!

POWPOWPOWPOWPOWPOWPOWPOW!

Miss Piggy snuggled up to her emerald prince. "Ooh, Kermie, you were so courageous, so magnificent!"

"I don't know what to say," shrugged Kermit, not knowing what to say.

"Say that the *bear* was magnificent," suggested Fozzie. "After all, *I* did all the driving."

"And *I* took a three-hundred-foot belly flop onto a moving car," Gonzo reminded them.

"Yes, but it was *Kermie* who took the Awesome Responsibility of Command," said Miss Piggy.

"I'm hungry," said Gonzo.

"I think we should check into a nice, quiet motel," suggested Miss Piggy. Her smokey blue eyes simmered. "Maybe we can have a quiet, little dinner...for two."

"Terrific!" said Gonzo, who felt he deserved some special treatment after his heroic act. "I'll eat with you, Miss Piggy."

Piggy whipped around and riveted Gonzo with a steely stare. "Not YOU, buzzard-beak," she snapped. She turned back to Kermit and her voice became a purr. "Just a nice, intimate dinner with...*mon capitaine.*"

The little station wagon barreled down the highway into the darkening twilight.

"I JUST GOTTA CATCH UP WITH THOSE GUYS!"

CHAPTER 7

Kermit the Frog sat nervously, waiting for his date to appear. The Terrace Restaurant at the Quiet Little Motel was a rustic spot with tiny dinner tables along a split-log railing that overlooked a lake with a waterwheel. The place was nice enough that one might just imagine having a romantic interlude there—but not one bit nicer. Kermit was decked out in a maroon velvet sports coat and an ascot, looking quite the cosmopolitan frog. As he sat listening to the softly lapping water, the door to the Terrace was flung open, and there, framed in the doorway, stood a vision awash in a sea of golden curls. Kermit was stunned.

"Well-well, good evening, Miss Piggy," he gulped. "You look lovely."

"Oh, thank you," she purred. "I'm sorry if I kept you waiting."

"It was worth it," said Kermit shyly. He hurried around the table to pull out her chair.

"Oh, *my*," she squealed, "how *charmant* of *vous*." A sour-looking waiter sauntered over.

"I took the liberty of ordering some wine," explained Kermit.

"Why you mad impetuous thing, you! It's champagne!"

"Not exactly," sneered the waiter. He fished an opener from his pocket and flipped off the bottlecap. "Sparkling muscatel," he informed them sarcastically, "one of the great wines of Idaho."

"It should be for ninety-five cents," said Kermit proudly as the waiter poured the wine. "That will be all for now," he added airily.

"Oh, thank you, sir! Thank you!" and with exaggerated bows, the waiter backed out of the room.

Kermit turned to Piggy, quite pleased with how he had handled the whole situation. "He's very good, isn't he?" he said admiringly.

But Piggy had eyes only for her frog. "Mmm-hmmm," she murmured.

"Well," Kermit raised his glass and stared deep into Miss Piggy's limpid blue eyes, "here's to you, Piggy."

Piggy tossed off her wine. "Ooh! It makes me all ... giggly!"

"The wine?"

Piggy paused.

"Everything," she sighed.

Kermit was transfixed. "Uh, it's a beautiful evening, isn't it?"

"Mmmm-hmmmm."

"... And... and the moon is just lovely."

"Mmmm-hmmmm."

Kermit was a goner. "But you know, Miss Piggy, the moon doesn't hold a candle to you."

The moon glinted silver on the surface of the lake. There was no sound but the lapping of the waves., Piggy and Kermit gazed deeply, passionately into each other's eyes. Slowly, inexorably, as if in the grip of some mighty magnet, they felt themselves drawn toward each other. Closer and closer until their lips were almost—

"Miss Piggy!" It was the waiter. "Miss Piggy! Phone call for Miss Piggy!" He looked coldly at the startled couple sitting by the railing. "Hey, you Miss Piggy?"

"Oh, dear, yes...." She turned to Kermit apologetically. "I ... I did place one little call to my agent, Kermit. I'll only be an eentsy-teentsy moment, I promise," and with a toss of her head she sprinted inside.

Kermit sighed and looked at the slowly turning waterwheel. "What the hey," he shrugged.

Time, as is its wont, passed. The shimmering moon sank lower, the candle on Kermit's table marked the passing hours by burning to a stub, and the waiter began stacking the chairs on top of the tables.

The forlorn frog finally got up to leave. "Here's the ninety-five cents for the wine," he said sadly to the waiter, handing him a dollar bill. "Keep the change."

The waiter studied the dollar for a moment. "Why is it always true," he muttered, "frogs are lousy tippers?"

Wondering what to do next, Kermit became aware of the tinkling of a distant piano. He wandered inside, where he found a pianist playing to an empty house.

"Evening. I'm Rowlf. Rowlf the Dog."

"Kermit, Kermit the Frog."

"Lemme guess…" said Rowlf, studying Kermit's woeful countenance, "broken heart, right?"

"Does it show?"

"Listen, greenhorn, when you've been tickling the ivories as long as I have, you've seen a broken heart for every drop of rain—a shattered dream for every fallen star."

Kermit sat down next to the piano. "She just…walked out on me."

"Typical," muttered Rowlf, shaking his head wearily. "That's why I live alone. I finish work, go home, read a book, have a couple of beers, take myself out for a walk, go to bed."

"Sounds nice and simple," said Kermit.

"Right. Stay away from women, that's my motto."

A loud voice from the kitchen interrupted them. "Kermit the Frog! Hey, phone call for Kermit the Frog!" The waiter appeared. He studied Kermit for a moment. "You Kermit the Frog?"

Kermit nodded to Rowlf and hurried off to get the call. Rowlf noodled a few notes and looked after him knowingly.

"It's not often you see a guy that green who's got the blues that bad."

"Hello?"

"Kermit!" a terrified female voice wailed from the receiver. "They've got me! Do anything they ask, please!"

"Piggy! Is that you?" The next voice Kermit heard made his heart sink even lower.

"That's her all right and this is Doc Hopper! Listen, Frog, and listen good: you step outside the motel right now! My guys will meet you there."

"And wh-what if I don't?"

"If you don't," cackled Doc, "your girlfriend will be hamhocks by breakfast! Now move!" Kermit hung up the phone. This whole evening had turned into a terrible nightmare. What could happen next?

Slowly he walked to the door and stepped outside.

"ARE YOU THE GUYS I'M SUPPOSED TO MEET?"

CHAPTER 8

Doc's hideout was an abandoned barn at the end of a winding dirt road. A single bare light bulb dangled from the ceiling.

Kermit and Miss Piggy were tightly bound to a wooden post in the middle of the room. Doc strolled around them, whistling merrily, as eight of his meanest-looking goons lounged around on bales of hay. They were obviously waiting for something.

Piggy leaned over to Kermit. "I want you to know," she whispered, "I'm not a bit worried. I know you are planning something bold and clever."

"Well," gulped Kermit, "I got us this far, didn't I?"

Max burst into the barn, accompanied by a small man with a shiny forehead and a mad gleam in his eye, wearing a white laboratory coat and high black boots. Doc ran over to greet him.

"Ahh, Professor Krassman, this is truly a pleasure! This," Doc turned gleefully to his captives, "is the world's leading authority on mind control in frogs!"

"It iss a rapidly growing field," hissed Krassman.

"Tell us what you're going to do to our little green friend here," gloated Doc.

"Vell, hold on to your hat," said Krassman. Doc smiled at him. Krassman was furious.

"Ven a German scientist says 'hold on to your hat,' hold on to your hat!" he screamed *"Hat! Hold!"*

Doc grabbed his hat in terror. "Good!" Krassman nodded approvingly. "Bring out the machine!" A machine was quickly wheeled into the shed, a sleek and frightening-looking device covered with dangling wires and blinking lights—and with a small seat that looked sickeningly like…an electric chair. Krassman caressed it lovingly. "Vait'll you see this," he crooned."You think ve're sleeping in Dusseldorf? No! Ve're vorking at night! Each night a new dial, a new knob, a new diode! Vhat does it do?" Krassman embraced the machine, practically drooling with rapture. "It turns the brain to"— he doubled over, convulsed for a moment in maniacal glee— "guacamole" Now he and Doc were both weeping with laughter. *"HALT!"* shouted Krassman, and the smile died on Doc's lips.

"Now," Krassman continued, "ve are going to strap the F-O-R-G into the little chair, drop the electronic skullcap and throw what ve call in German, Der SVITCH! Then the frog vill do your bidding, he vill do your commercials, he vill *sell your frogs' legs!* Ha, ha, ha, haha!"

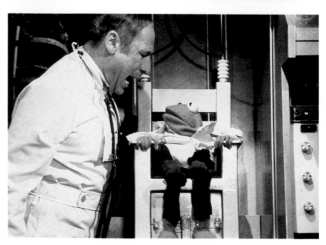

"OKAY, *PIG*, SAY GOOD-BYE TO THE FROG!"

Krassman wheeled and fixed his insane stare on the two terrified prisoners. "Alright, Kermick! Bring the Kermick over here!"

Piggy was indignant. "That's Ker*mit*," she snapped. "With a *T*."

"Please," gulped the frog in question, "don't help him."

"Put him in the chair!" barked Krassman. "Let's blow his brains out!"

"Kermit," whispered Piggy, "whatever happens next, I just want you to know I wouldn't give up this evening together for anything in the world. Would you?"

"Make me an offer," croaked Kermit miserably.

Two of the thugs untied Kermit and dragged him over to Krassman's terrible machine. They threw him onto the seat and strapped him down.

"Okay, Pig, say good-bye to the frog!" leered Krassman.

"Wh-why should I?" Piggy quavered.

"Because," Krassman laughed, "his brain is about to go bye-bye. After I throw 'der svitch,' he von't know you from … kosher bacon!" Grinning crazily, Krassman reached slowly for the awful lever. Piggy had had enough. "That does it," she muttered. Taking a deep breath, she strained against the ropes.

"HI-YAAAH!"

"HI-YAAAH!"

The terrible war cry resounded through the barn and for an instant all its occupants were frozen in fear. An instant was all it took. The ropes which bound Miss Piggy to the post snapped like thread, unleashing her in all her fury. Eyes blazing like those of a thing possessed, she rocketed across the barn, catching Krassman square in the gut with a devastating karate kick. As the startled scientist crumpled before her onslaught, the enraged pig wheeled upon Hopper's hired henchmen.

"HI-YAAAH!" The pink tornado ripped through the rank of startled thugs, scattering them in her wake. One of them dove for a shotgun.

"HI-YAAAH!" The gun was wrenched from his hands and wrapped around his neck. Two of Hopper's men charged her from behind. They had clubs.

"HI-YAAAH!" The thugs never got a chance to use them. Two smashing karate chops sent them spinning across the barn, bringing rakes and hoes crashing down around them. Three more men leaped on her...and were tossed away like bean bags.

"HI-YAAAH!"

Krassman, gasping for breath, pulled himself toward the awful machine, his face set in a grimace of insane determination.

"Got to get to the machine," he gasped, "must reach…'der SVITCH.'"

Piggy turned just in time. OOMPH! Another lethal kick caught the mad professor just as he grasped the lever. Back into the machine he toppled, knocking aside Kermit as he fell. There was a blinding flash of light and a ghastly electronic crackle as Krassman stood caught in the machine's awful forces. Finally he tore himself away and staggered forward, his face contorted in a blank, uncomprehending stare, his brain, undoubtedly, turned to guacamole.

"Ribbit," he croaked, "Ribbit, ribbit," and fell with a crash to the floor.

"Ribit Ribit"

The next morning, several miles from the barn, an angry Doc Hopper stood outside his black limousine, talking to an oddly dressed man. The newcomer wore a jet black diving suit crisscrossed with bands of murderous-looking tridents, a black hat and dark glasses. He carried a spear gun. "This is Snake Walker, Max. Tell Max what you do, Snake." Snake narrowed his eyes and spat. His reply was succinct…

"Kill frogs"

CHAPTER 9

The station wagon rolled smoothly westward along the desert highway. Kermit was happy to be back on the road again, leaving behind all the craziness of the night before. Rowlf the piano player had decided to come with them to Hollywood, and Kermit figured they would just make the auditions… if nothing else went wrong.

Far down the highway they could see a hitchhiker by the roadside. As they drew closer, Fozzie slowed the station wagon. The hitchhiker was standing next to a large suitcase and waving frantically. She wore high heels and fishnet stockings and…. Kermit slapped his forehead in disbelief as she ran up to the passenger side of the car.

"Kermie! What an unbelievable coincidence! It's so good to see you again! And there's just enough room up front for me to snuggle next to you!" Miss Piggy heaved her suitcase into the back and climbed in.

"Ooh, Kermie, don't I even get one little kiss?"

"No."

There was a crackle of static on the car radio and the music was suddenly interrupted by a voice that made Kermit's blood run cold.

"This is Doc Hopper here, saying that if Kermit the Frog doesn't stop and call me right now and agree to be my national spokesman, he will soon find his legs rolled in bread crumbs. The toll-free number is…."

Kermit snapped off the radio and stared out the window. They were in the middle of the desert. There was no one around for miles and nothing but smooth highway between them and Hollywood. They were home free—unless something happened to the car.

"I JUST GOTTA CATCH UP WITH THOSE GUYS!"

With a sickening sputter, the little station wagon jerked
forward twice and stopped dead in its tracks.
"Oh boy, Kermit," observed Fozzie, "I think we're in trouble."

Cool night air settled over the desert as the six dejected travelers huddled around their small campfire. Only the occasional crackling of the flames broke the silence.

"Well," Rowlf finally said, "I guess we blew it."

Gonzo was staring up at the clear, star-filled sky. "Yeah," he said wistfully, "but it sure is beautiful out here. You could get lost in a sky like that. I wish I had those balloons again."

"Kermit, we... we're gonna miss those auditions, right?" Fozzie asked. Kermit said nothing for a moment.

"Look, gang," he finally answered, "I never promised we'd make it. I never promised... anything!" He got up and walked away from the fire, too unhappy to say anything else. The others watched Kermit's little figure disappear into the desert. What could they say? Rowlf reached under his covers and pulled out a harmonica. A mournful tune wafted through the still night air. Gonzo looked up at the stars and began to sing.

This looks familiar,
Vaguely familiar,
Almost unreal yet
It's too soon to feel yet,
Close to my soul and yet
So far away...
I'm going to go back there some day.
Some day...

Sun rises, night falls,
Sometimes the sky calls,

Is that a song there?
I've never been there,
But I know the way...
I'm going to go back there some day.

Come and go with me
It's more fun to share,
We'll both be completely at home
In midair!
We're flying not riding
On featherless wings
We can hold on to love
Like invisible strings.

There's not a word yet
For old friends who've just met,
Part heaven, part space
Or have I found my place,
You can just visit
But I plan to stay...
I'm going to go back there some day.

Kermit wandered on into the desert. The soft music around the campfire faded into the distance.

"*Why?*" he asked himself. "*Why? I didn't promise any-one anything.... What do I know about Hollywood, anyway?*" He sat down on a rock and tried to sort things out in his mind. "*So why did I leave the swamp?*

'Because some agent fellow said I have talent. He probably says that to everybody.

'Of course, if I hadn't come, I'd be feeling pretty miserable too.
'Yeah, but it would just be *me* feeling miserable. Now I've got a lady pig and a bear and a chicken and a—whatever Gonzo is—and a dog all feeling miserable. I brought 'em all out here into the middle of nowhere.

'Whether I promised them something or not, they wanted to come.
'But that's because they believed in me.

'No. They believed in the dream." Kermit was staring straight up at the stars.

"So do I, but…
"You do? Well then?" There was a sudden blaze of light as a shooting star streaked across the sky.

"I was wrong when I said I never promised anyone," Kermit said "I promised *me*."

The moment Kermit said those words aloud, he felt his confidence return. They could make it, he was sure. There *must* be a way. He turned and headed back to the campfire. As he drew nearer, he became aware that something was different, something had changed. He heard music, but it wasn't the sad sound of Rowlf's harmonica. It was a wild, pounding sound like…

Kermit hurried over a rise and looked down on the campfire. Parked next to it, the glow of the firelight dancing on its wildly decorated sides, was an old school bus. And sitting around the fire was an equally wild-looking group of musicians.

"Doctor Teeth! Janice! Scooter! Floyd! Zoot! Animal!" With a whoop of delight, Kermit ran down to join them. "I'm...I'm amazed! How did you guys find us."

Doctor Teeth held up the copy of the movie script Kermit and Fozzie had left back at the church. "Hey," he chuckled, "we just read ahead in the script until we came to the place where it says, 'Exterior–Desert–Night: Cool night air settles over the desert as...' When do you gotta be at those auditions?"

"Two o'clock tomorrow afternoon."

"Well, climb aboard! We'll have breakfast at Hollywood and Vine."

As the others rushed aboard the bus, Kermit lingered for a moment and looked up at the beautiful night sky. "I promised me," he softly repeated.

CHAPTER 10

The bus sped down the smooth asphalt strip of highway and into the glare of the western morning. Most of the passengers slept. Kermit, however, sat in the rear, staring out the back window, thinking about what lay ahead. Miss Piggy sat next to him, but her mind was on other things.

"Kermit?"

"Oh, hi." Kermit's thoughts seemed far away.

"Oh, Kermie, whisper sweet nothings into my ear."

"Hmmm... motorcycle cop."

"That's a sweet nothing?"

"No, a motorcycle cop is chasing us!" Miss Piggy looked out the window just in time to see the policeman swing his motorcycle parallel with the bus and signal for it to pull over.

"Hey, Doctor Teeth, you'd better stop," called Kermit.

Doctor Teeth pulled the bus over to the side of the road, and the officer climbed off his bike and slowly walked toward them. He wore a shiny helmet with a plastic visor that totally obscured his face.

"Uh, did we do something wrong, sir?" Kermit asked respectfully. The cop climbed into the bus and suddenly flipped up his visor. A gasp of surprise and fear ran through the bus.

"It's him, Kermit!" yelled Fozzie. "It's Doc Hopper's assistant!"

"Wait!" pleaded Max, "hear me out, *please!*"

"Okay, gang," said Kermit, "let him talk."

"I'm here to warn you," Max said earnestly. "Doc's mad now. He's right behind you, and he's ready to do anything!"

"Time to beat feet," Floyd suggested. "Let's move it, Kermit."

"Look, I want to help," Max continued. "Don't stay on the highway! If you stay on the highway, he'll definitely catch you."

Kermit stood thinking for a moment. "Fine," he said at last. "Doctor Teeth, what's up the road straight ahead of us?"

"Just some old ghost town, Froggie."

"OK," said Kermit, "we'll pull in there and wait for him." The others stared at him in amazement.

Kermit turned to his friends. "Let me explain, gang," he said quietly, "I can't spend my whole life being chased by a bully. Max, you go tell Doc where I'll be.

"Look, everyone," he continued, "I know you're counting on getting to those auditions. I know that's why you're here. If I spoil your dream, I'm sorry. But I have to do this."

Everyone was quiet for a long moment, then Fozzie spoke up.

"I understand, Kermit."

"I'll stand with you," added Gonzo.

"We all will," said Scooter.

"We're with our friend the frog," agreed Floyd.

"BEAT DRUM!" yelled Animal. It was unanimous.

Kermit looked around gratefully at all his friends. "To the ghost town!" he announced.

A few minutes later, Doctor Teeth parked the bus on the deserted street that led through the middle of the ghost town. Kermit stared at the weathered buildings and battered signs. The place looked just like an old abandoned movie set.

"I'm going to look around," said Kermit. "Everybody stay in the bus."

"Hey, Kermit," called Floyd, "can I take Animal for a walk? He needs his exercise."

"Sure, go ahead." Kermit looked up and down the street. Nearby was what appeared to be an old general store. Not much there—a few broken chairs and a wooden rain barrel…with a blast of tinny music, the rain barrel suddenly sprang to life.

"What the hey…?" Kermit almost leaped out of his skin. The barrel was spinning rapidly and playing a frantic version of "Lady of Spain." What kind of place was this?

A peculiar, high-pitched voice greeted Kermit. "Good day, sir. You are enjoying one of my latest inventions—the revolving musical rain barrel!" Two heads had appeared around the corner of the general store and were staring at the startled frog. The speaker was a small fellow in a lab coat who rather reminded Kermit of a melon wearing glasses. His bug-eyed companion seemed capable of communicating only in nervous squeaks.

"Who would want a revolving musical rain barrel?" asked Kermit quite sensibly.

"What an odd question," remarked the inventor. "I am Doctor Bunsen Honeydew and this is my assistant, Beaker. We live here perfecting useful inventions. Come in, come in." Kermit walked a little uncertainly into the store, followed by Floyd and Animal.

"Hey, like what are you dudes *doin'* here?" Floyd asked.

"I'm *so* glad you asked," chirped Bunsen. "We are, in fact, perfecting our latest invention, Insta-Grow pills!" He pointed to a jar sitting on the counter, but Floyd couldn't help noticing the huge, wrinkled black and purple mess that sat next to it.

"What in the name of Fats Waller is *that*?" he gasped.

"A four-foot prune, of course," Bunsen answered matter-of-factly.

Animal was poking curiously at the jar. "What else will these pills make big?" Floyd asked.

"Oh, anything," replied Bunsen, "but the effect is, sadly, only temporary."

"KERMIT! KERMIT!" Scooter was yelling frantically from the bus. "Here comes Doc Hopper!"

This was it. Kermit braced himself for the final showdown.

FOUR-FOOT PRUNE

The grim green figure strode out of the storefront porch's shadow, his steely eyes glinting in the dusty town's harsh sunlight, bright as the spurs on his boots. The ten-pint hat he wore made him look proud and tall as he slowly walked into the street. A frog's gotta do what a frog's gotta do.

The all-too-familiar black limousine which was heading in Kermit's direction came to a screeching halt. Its doors swung open ominously, and out stepped Doc Hopper, Max and the man in the black wetsuit, Snake Walker, the Frogkiller.

Behind them a battered pickup truck clattered to a stop, and out piled six of the meanest, ugliest, orneriest gun-toting goons a frog could ever do battle with.

"Alright, Frog," yelled Doc down the long stretch of street. "One last chance: Are you going to do my commercials live or—" he grinned horribly—"stuffed?" His henchmen laughed and cocked their shotguns, and the Frogkiller, with an evil grin, shoved a spiked trident into his spear gun.

"Hopper, what's the matter with you?" Kermit yelled back. "You gotta be crazy, chasing me halfway across the country like this. Why do you have to do this to me?"

Doc hadn't expected this. He stopped abruptly. A gust of desert wind stirred the dust on the street and sent a couple of tumbleweeds skittering past. "Because all my life I wanted to own a thousand frogs' legs restaurants and you're the key, greenie."

"Well," Kermit began slowly, "maybe you can own all those restaurants, Hopper. But there are some things your money will never buy."

"Oh yeah? Like what?"

Kermit paused for a moment, then fixed his level gaze on Doc. He spoke clearly and deliberately, his voice rising as he answered.

"Did you ever see a rainbow, Doc? You can't buy it, or kidnap it, or put it in a cage or have it stuffed, because it's there for everybody and nobody can own it.

"You know, Doc, we're not all that different. I've got a dream too, but mine's about singing and dancing and making people happy. That's the kind of dream that gets better the more people you share it with, and I've found a whole bunch of people who have the same dream—it makes us kind of a family. Do you have anyone like that, Doc? Once you get all those restaurants, who you gonna share them with? Who are your friends, Doc? These guys?"

Doc looked at his unsavory crew. "I got lots of friends," he said loudly. "...Uh, Max for instance." He grinned desperately at Max, who quietly shook his head. "No, Doc." he said, "you lost me a long time ago."

Doc looked stunned.

"I don't think you're a bad man, Doc." Kermit continued. "And I think that if you look into your heart, you'll find you really want to let me and my friends go, to follow our dream. But if that's not the kind of man you are—" Kermit lowered his head and his voice, "—then go ahead and kill me."

Doc was practically trembling with emotion at Kermit's words. As he tried to keep his composure, a tear ran down the end of his nose and fell onto his white jacket. He knew now what he had to do. With great difficulty and resignation, he spoke to the seven men behind him.

"All right, boys," he said. "Kill him."

The Frogkiller and the goons began marching slowly and murderously down the street. Kermit and his friends stood shaking with terror. The very ground seemed to be shaking with them… in fact, it was! A strange, low rumbling sound filled the air. Doc's men stopped in confusion. The sound became louder and louder, growing into a terrifying, blood-curdling roar. It seemed to be coming from the old general store. Everyone turned to stare in awe and trembling fear.

"LOOK!" screamed Doc.
"THE ROOF! IT'S...EXPLODING!"

The store roof shattered into a thousand pieces as a huge head burst through it, *fifteen feet across!* It was Animal! Out came his shoulders, wide as a six-lane highway. The gigantic figure hovered demonically over the tiny people below, covering half the town with its shadow. He looked down at the figures of Doc and his men, opened his mouth and roared. The blast of his breath sent them somersaulting down the street like clumps of tumbleweed. Screaming with terror, they picked themselves up and, as fast as they could, falling over each other in their panic, they ran off into the desert.

The overjoyed travelers hopped up and down and hugged each other, as Animal, shrunk back to his normal size, stomped out of the store. There was nothing to stop them now!

"Okay, everybody" cried Kermit the Frog, "on to Hollywood!"

CHAPTER 11

Kermit and his friends marched into the outer suite of Lew Lord's Hollywood offices. Lew Lord, kingpin of Wide World Studios, one of the most powerful men in Hollywood! Kermit wondered what he would be like.

His place certainly was impressive! The magnificent ceilings were at least twenty feet high, and the walls were covered with obviously expensive artwork and sculpture. And this was just his secretary's office! Everyone was overwhelmed.

"Oh, Kermie," gasped Miss Piggy, "this is like a dream come true!"

"Well, don't count your tadpoles 'til they're hatched," Kermit warned everyone. "I've still got to audition."

"Don't worry," Floyd said encouragingly. "*You* can cut it, greenstuff." Their feet sank into the lush white rug as they made their way across the enormous anteroom toward the massive, slightly open oaken doors that led to Lew Lord's private office. At that moment Lew Lord's secretary finally noticed them.

"You can't go in there!" She was outraged. "Mr. Lord is busy packaging a blockbuster!" She quickly pressed a button on her desk and the mighty doors closed with a thud in Kermit's face.

"But... but I'm here to audition for Mr. Lord!" Kermit couldn't believe it. Had they come this far, struggled through such dangers, only to be stopped just short of their goal?

"You can't just come in here off the street," the secretary was saying smugly, "especially with all these…" she looked at Kermit's crew as if seeing them for the first time, "… these…*animals!*"

"And what's wrong with *animals?*" demanded Kermit.

"Well, for one thing," Kermit noticed that the secretary's eyes were watering and she was trying to suppress a sneeze, "I'm…I'm allergic to, to…Ah…Ah…animal—SPLCHOO! hair. Now get them ou… ou…OWBSLCHH of here before I ca…ca…CACHOO!"

**"ACK-AH-OH-OHohohHOOSH!
ApstLOOH!
Hackahacka, OH!
AhHOOEY!"**

This was a desperate moment and it called for desperate measures. Kermit reached over and flicked on the fan in the corner. The breeze riffled through Animal's hair and sent a flurry of fuzz and fur drifting toward the secretary.

"…Before I ca…ca…call security ACK-AH-OH-OHohohHOOSH! AbspLOOH! Hackahacka, Oh! P-please get them AhHOOEY!" Wracked by fits of sneezes the woman collapsed on the desk, looking imploringly at Kermit the Frog. Grimly Kermit directed another blast of fur and feathers in her direction. Slowly the woman slid off the desk onto the floor behind, until all that could be seen of her was one limply waving hand signaling them

toward the doors to Lew Lord's office. The hand fell upon the button, and with a clunk and a whir, the doors majestically swung open.

"This is it, gang," Kermit said solemnly. He took a deep breath and walked straight up to the palatial desk where Lew Lord sat, his back to the intruders.

"Mr. Lord," Kermit announced boldly, "forgive the interruption, but I demand an audition!"

"Yeah!" said Floyd.

"You tell him, Kermit!" added Fozzie.

"I've come two thousand miles," Kermit continued confidently, "I've been chased by a crazy guy with a French Fried Fr—…uh…oh, boy!" Kermit's voice trailed away in awe.

Lew Lord slowly swiveled in his chair to face them. He was a huge man with a great gray beard and eyes that could melt steel. An enormous cigar protruded from his mouth. From beneath his beetling brows he stared silently at Kermit and his companions. Kermit stepped back, seeking protection from his friends.

"We're with you, Kermie," said Miss Piggy quietly. Kermit swallowed hard and spoke again, hesitantly, looking straight at the imposing man who held their future in his hands.

"P-p-please, sir, I'm K-Kermit the Frog. We…we've seen your ad and…we've come to Hollywood to be," he gulped again "…rich and famous." Lew Lord studied each of them for a moment, and his eyes seemed to burn through their very souls. The room was deathly silent as the trembling group stood before him, waiting for some answer, some sign. Finally a faint smile crossed his lips. Or was it a sneer? Either way his mind was made up. He shifted the huge cigar slightly in his mouth, then, slowly, Lew Lord, the mightiest mogul in Hollywood history, reached for his intercom button.

"Miss Tracey," he said into the intercom—his rich, bell-like voice reverberated through the silent room— "prepare the standard 'Rich and Famous' contract for Kermit the Frog and Company."

"We did it!
WE DID IT!"

WORLD WIDE STUDIOS
RICH AND FAMOUS CONTRACT

WHEREAS, rcwigh mnpr uf pkltvbdwr yhg known as, Kermit the Frog, Fozzie the Bear, Miss Piggy and friends (herein, the talent) and World Wide Studios (herein, the studio) resolve to waesfkj fb yfpmbncfk ds wdnothp this wxdroihrdnl ref 1979. Gnfpg erd mnhoesde hgpt motion picture bvrt and the talent powsdh irgt.

(a) wrjkt fop tropjwdth Kermit wdpj ot nmgpoegh czdi ga outgyws cdi.

(b) hjrevi ha cdore Miss Piggy cotfkts rtuyhowdcs wdlo om wrdtiet rfuab.

(c) Fozzie Bear tyhuedf rpo tfejikln wdsiujlbg et tsu rdoli wesd edcfjillkmj ye.

WHEREAS, rdskojmkr tge wrdujo dfe the talent and the studio wrduko rohg jlkitgfk shall endeavor to wrkpolfe rdwe rtedji rich and famous.

(a) Zyhfgcd jtlo ytgec edli rytokhr gtkojedsc fro goknaf.

(b) RWJPLD gytjvdem qxfo pka Kermit esfwih ry dtihav rseki.

IN WITNESS WHEREOF, the parties hereto have duly executed this agreement.

WORLD WIDE STUDIOS

Witness: _Sally Bass_

Lew Lord
Lew Lord, President

Witness: _(signature)_

Kermit the Frog
Kermit the Frog

Witness: _ANIMAL_

Fozzie
Fozzie Bear

Witness: _Betty Ballantine_

Miss Piggy xx
Miss Piggy

THE
MUPPET
MOVIE
Shooting Script

THE
MUPPET
MOVIE
Shooting Script

1. INTERIOR—ENORMOUS HOLLYWOOD SOUNDSTAGE—DAY:

In a LONG SHOT from high above, we SEE a small green figure sitting alone on a high stool in the middle of the studio. It is KERMIT THE FROG, apparently lost in thought. Up-tempo MUSIC begins as the CAMERA, in a long, gliding shot, zooms in to a close-up of Kermit. He SINGS:

KERMIT

It starts when we're kids,
A show-off at school,
Makin' faces at friends,
You're a clown and a fool...

2. Kermit gets up and DANCES to his right. The CAMERA FOLLOWS him as he continues to sing...

Doin' pratfalls and birdcalls
And bad imitations,
Ignorin' your homework
(Is that dedication?)...

3. He STOPS between two MAKE-UP MIRRORS. They face each other so that AN INFINITY OF KERMITS is reflected in them.

You work to the mirror,
Getting standing ovations!

SCOOTER AND ROBIN (on next cart)
What was once juvenilish...

PIGGY (on same cart, appearing from behind wardrobe rack dressed in a glamorous gown)
Is grown-up and stylish...

4. LONG SHOT of huge studio
   doors. FOZZIE drives in in a
   small TRACTOR towing four
   flatbed TRAILERS over-
   flowing with PROPS, MOVIE-
   MAKING EQUIPMENT and the
   rest of the cast. As their
   cars pass by, they continue
   the song:

FOZZIE
You're burning with hope...

ELECTRIC MAYHEM (on first cart)
You're building up steam...

GONZO, CAMILLA, BUNSEN,
BEAKER, ROWLF
(on final cart)
You're close to your dream!

5. An ARC LIGHT swings around
   and focuses on KERMIT.
   Others continue to sing...
   ALL
   Then somebody out there
   loves you,
   Stands up and
   hollers for more—

FOZZIE (standing up and hollering)
<u>More!!!</u>

ALL
<u>You've found a home in the magic store!</u>

ANIMAL jumps off the trailer, yanking over FLOYD who is holding his chain.

FLOYD
Hey! Whoa! Halt! Cease! Desist! Stop...

JANICE (carrying letters of Hollywood sign)
Wow, like let's do it!

ZOOT (vaguely)
Do what?

7. Up-tempo MUSIC continues
   as camera PANS along the
   line of TRAILERS. Cast
   members SPEAK as camera
   passes:

KERMIT (importantly)
Okay, everybody. Let's get
the number together!

DR. TEETH (to his group)
Off the truck and on the job!

SCOOTER
(carrying large sign reading
THE MOVIES)
The movie!
PIGGY
Makeup!

8. KERMIT in director's chair
KERMIT
Fozzie, get those wagons out
of here!

9. FOZZIE at wheel of tractor
FOZZIE
Yes,SIR! <u>Movin' right
along...</u>

10. CAMERA continues to follow
frenzied activity. MAYHEM
are setting up large cut-
out of their CHURCH,

FOZZIE
is positioning a cardboard
replica of his STUDEBAKER,

11. KERMIT in director's chair
KERMIT
You look beautfiul, Miss
Piggy! (aside) That's
Hollywood talk.

12. FOZZIE carries in an EL
SLEEZO CAFE SIGN and helps
ROWLF set up the CAMERA.
The last SETS are pushed
into place, and the cy-
clorama, a huge painted
BACKDROP, is raised. Ev-
erything is ready for the
making of THE MUPPET MOVIE.
SCOOTER holds up the slate.

GONZO goes by carrying a
cutout of his BALLOONS,

PIGGY is at the make-up
mirror, having her hair
styled by BEAKER.

SCOOTER
Action!
He slams it on his finger
Owwwww!

13. CRAZY HARRY cackles and
slowly pushes up the LEVERS
on the huge LIGHT BOARD
that turn on the enormous
MOVIE LIGHTS...

... LUSH MUSIC
swells and KERMIT moves
into the set. The TREES
behind him look a great
deal like his old SWAMP. He
begins to sing...
KERMIT
<u>Why are there so many
Songs about rainbows?</u>

Kermit crosses to his RIGHT,
meeting FOZZIE in front of
the EL SLEEZO sign.
FOZZIE
<u>That's part of what rainbows do...</u>

The MAYHEM go by in their
bus, as others SET UP the
HOLLYWOOD sign.
ALL
<u>All of us watching and
wishing we'd find it,</u>

KERMIT (to camera)
<u>I know that you're watching, too.</u>

Kermit continues to cross,
meeting PIGGY in front of
the COUNTY FAIR set. Between
them is GONZO, clutching his
cardboard cutout balloons. A
heavy ROPE begins to haul
him up into the air.
GONZO
Rainbows are memories...

PIGGY puts her arm around
KERMIT
PIGGY
Sweet dream reminders,
What is it you'd like to do?

Entire CAST is now standing
in front of huge cutout
rainbow. KERMIT and PIGGY
are hand in hand in the
foreground as the MUSIC
soars toward a glorious
FINALE...
ALL
Someday we'll find it,
The rainbow connection,
The lovers, the dreamers and...

CAMERA follows GONZO as he
swings joyfully through the
sky on his cardboard
balloons.
GONZO
Ya-HOOO...OO...

"…Oops!"

With a thud, Gonzo and his balloons swung up against the gigantic wooden rainbow that arched across the studio. For one long agonizing moment there was a shuddering silence, and then, with a heartrending crunch, the great rainbow slowly began to topple. Faster and faster it fell, smashing against the other parts of the set as it came, bringing them crashing down like a house of cards. Down came the swamp, the Ferris wheel and the church, the bus, the Studebaker and the El Sleezo Cafe. Down came the giant backdrop and the Hollywood hills. Kermit and Piggy clung to each other in terror as an enormous chunk of scenery bounced past them and into Crazy Harry's light board. It hit with a shower of sparks and a blinding flash of light. All over the studio the huge movie lights began to explode, first the ones on the floor, then, with a terrible roar, the lights on the ceiling, blowing an enormous hole in the roof. The room filled with smoke and falling plaster.

Kermit and his friends stared upward through the settling smoke and dust at the hole in the roof. A shaft of sunlight seemed to be struggling to pierce its way through. The smoke swirled and settled, and the beam of light arc'ed overhead, curving across the studio in a great and glorious rainbow.

15. CAMERA in TIGHT on KERMIT and PIGGY, slowly starts to PULL BACK. KERMIT begins to sing, softly.

KERMIT
Life's like a movie,
Write your own ending...

CAMERA continues to PULL BACK, revealing FOZZIE, GONZO, CAMILLA, ROWLF and THE ELECTRIC MAYHEM. They join in.

Keep believing, keep pretending...

By now the camera has pulled
back to HIGH ABOVE the
studio floor, revealing
literally HUNDREDS of
MUPPETS massed together in a
great pool of light at the
end of the glowing rainbow.
Their voices, joining
together, swell in a final
chorus...

<u>We've done</u> <u>just what we set</u>
<u>out to do!</u>
<u>Thanks to the lovers.</u>
<u>The dreamers...</u>
<u>And you!</u>

—THE END—

"I JUST KNEW I'D CATCH UP WITH YOU GUYS!"